HIP-HOP
ARTISTS

THE WEEKND

R&B MEGASTAR

BY ERIN NICKS

Essential Library

An Imprint of Abdo Publishing
abdobooks.com

ABDOBOOKS.COM

Published by Abdo Publishing, a division of ABDO, PO Box 398166, Minneapolis, Minnesota 55439. Copyright © 2022 by Abdo Consulting Group, Inc. International copyrights reserved in all countries. No part of this book may be reproduced in any form without written permission from the publisher. Essential Library™ is a trademark and logo of Abdo Publishing.

Printed in the United States of America, North Mankato, Minnesota.
102021
012022

THIS BOOK CONTAINS
RECYCLED MATERIALS

Cover Photo: Kevin Mazur/Getty Images for TW/Getty Images
Interior Photos: Steve Luciano/AP Images, 4; Aaron Doster/AP Images, 6–7; Ashley Landis/AP Images, 9; Leonard Zhukovsky/Shutterstock Images, 11; Lev Radin/Shutterstock Images, 13; Jai Agnish/Shutterstock Images, 14; Stephane Legrand/Shutterstock Images, 16; Edmond Sadaka Edmond/Sipa/AP Images, 18; Shutterstock Images, 20, 70, 75, 76; Everett Atlas/Shutterstock Images, 22; Jamie Lamor Thompson/Shutterstock Images, 24; Clinton Gilders/FilmMagic/Getty Images, 26; John Steel/Shutterstock Images, 29; Christian Bertrand/Shutterstock Images, 31, 90; Sonia Recchia/WireImage/Getty Images, 32–33; Tsugufumi Matsumoto/AP Images, 34; Frazer Harrison/Getty Images for Coachella/Getty Images Entertainment/Getty Images, 36; Ian West/AP Images, 38; Vince Talotta/Toronto Star/Getty Images, 41; Vallery Jean/WireImage/Getty Images, 44; Sean Thompson/AP Images, 45; Alexandra Wyman/Invision for Universal Music Group/AP Images, 48; Matt Sayles/Invision/AP Images, 50, 58–59, 62; Benjamin Shmikler/ABImages/AP Images, 52; Debby Wong/Shutterstock Images, 54; Scott Roth/Invision/AP Images, 56; Kathy Hutchins/Shutterstock Images, 60; Jon Elswick/AP Images, 65; Alberto E. Tamargo/Sipa USA/AP Images, 66; Kevin Mazur/WireImage/Getty Images, 72; Richard Shotwell/Invision/AP Images, 78; Jordan Crosby/Shutterstock Images, 80; Chris Pizzello/Invision/AP Images, 82, 89; Kobby Dagan/Shutterstock Images, 84; Kailin Huang/Shutterstock Images, 87; Owen Sweeney/Invision/AP Images, 94; Ric Tapia/AP Images, 96–97

Editor: Arnold Ringstad
Series Designer: Laura Graphenteen

LIBRARY OF CONGRESS CONTROL NUMBER: 2021941093
PUBLISHER'S CATALOGING-IN-PUBLICATION DATA

Names: Nicks, Erin, author.
Title: The Weeknd: R&B megastar / by Erin Nicks
Other title: R&B megastar
Description: Minneapolis, Minnesota : Abdo Publishing, 2022 | Series: Hip-hop artists | Includes online resources and index.
Identifiers: ISBN 9781532196195 (lib. bdg.) | ISBN 9781098218003 (ebook)
Subjects: LCSH: Weeknd, 1990- (Abel Tesfaye)--Juvenile literature. | Rap musicians--United States--Biography--Juvenile literature. | Rap (Music)--Juvenile literature. | Lyricists--Biography--Juvenile literature.
Classification: DDC 782.421649--dc23

CONTENTS

THE WEEKND AT HALFTIME

In the middle of a worldwide pandemic, one of the biggest musical stars on the planet was onstage in front of a massive audience, and no one quite knew what to expect. Abel Tesfaye, better known as The Weeknd, was seated in a vintage 1955 Mercedes-Benz 300 SL. He got out of the car and sat atop a gargantuan cube outlined in neon. He appeared to be taking time to absorb the weight of the moment.

Just under 100 million Americans were viewing Super Bowl LV on television, along with millions more watching around the world. Normally the stadium is packed full for these performances. But due to the physical distancing required by the COVID-19 pandemic, Raymond James Stadium in Tampa, Florida, held less than 40 percent of its usual capacity of 65,890. As the lights dimmed to indicate the start of the halftime show, 25,000 people sat

The Weeknd dazzled a global audience with his performance at the Super Bowl in 2021.

Empty seats dotted the arena, which had limited attendance due to the ongoing pandemic.

in the dark, waiting for the R&B singer from Scarborough, Ontario, to begin his performance.[1]

UNDER THE BLINDING LIGHTS

A choir began to sing the chorus of "Call Out My Name," one of the songs from The Weeknd's *My Dear Melancholy*.

Then the choir's stage divided in half, and The Weeknd emerged from the opening and launched into another one of his hits, "Starboy." Dressed in a black shirt, tie, pants, and gloves, a red crystal suit jacket, and two-tone wing tip shoes, the star ran through nine of his songs in

COVERING COSTS

The Weeknd's Super Bowl performance required six months of planning and preparation. He also contributed $7 million of his own money to create the show he wanted.[2] The NFL does not pay musical guests to appear during the halftime show, but the league does cover an undisclosed amount of production costs. The 2020 halftime show, which featured Shakira and Jennifer Lopez, is estimated to have cost $13 million.[3] Artists can see a bump in album sales immediately after a Super Bowl performance as a result of the massive exposure. On February 7, 2021, the day of Super Bowl LV, The Weeknd saw his sales spike up 385 percent over the previous day's.[4]

the nearly 15-minute set. A cameraman ran ahead of him as The Weeknd maneuvered through a maze of lights while crooning the song "Can't Feel My Face."

A multitude of dancers with red jackets and bandaged faces surrounded The Weeknd in the maze and followed as he descended from the stage and made his way onto the field. It was a callback to the singer's decision to cover most of his head in medical gauze for an appearance at the American Music Awards in November 2020. As the set wrapped with "Blinding Lights," Canada's biggest R&B star stood with arms outstretched, looking skyward as the crowd roared and fireworks exploded above.

KEEPING IT PG

The Super Bowl halftime show is one of the most prominent stages in the world, and the National Football League (NFL) tends to be extremely cautious about whom it

"There wasn't any room to fit it in the narrative, in the story I was telling in the performance. So yeah. There's no special guests."[5]

—The Weeknd on his decision to perform the entire halftime show on his own

Bandaged dancers surrounded The Weeknd during part of his flashy performance.

DRAWING UPON THE LEGENDS

When creating his halftime show performance, The Weeknd wanted to recall other memorable Super Bowl shows from artists he admired. During a press conference prior to the big game, he mentioned Prince, Michael Jackson, and Beyoncé as the musical talents from whom he was hoping to draw inspiration. He also referenced Diana Ross's halftime performance from 1996 as his favorite. "[Ross is] just so glamorous and the show just makes me smile," The Weeknd said. "And she has a great exit with the helicopter—it lands in the middle of the field, she grabs onto it and flies off into the clouds, it's like. . . . I wish I could have done that, I wish I'd thought of it. Although I don't think I have enough money to do it!"[7]

selects to perform there. The Weeknd is no stranger to controversy. The singer has included explicit references to drugs and sex in his lyrics. But he also has a massive mainstream following and a rabid fan base. The Weeknd was also conscious enough of his material to assure the audience at a pre–Super Bowl press conference that he would keep the show on the tamer side of things. "I definitely want to be respectful to the viewers at home," The Weeknd said.[6]

In addition to hosting the halftime show, The Weeknd participated in the Super Bowl experience in other ways. The halftime show was sponsored by the soft drink giant Pepsi, and

ADJUSTING TO PANDEMIC RULES

Performing in the middle of a pandemic presented an unprecedented set of challenges for The Weeknd, his accompanying singers and dancers, and everyone else involved with the show's production. More than 1,000 people, including onstage talent and on-site staff, needed to be constantly tested and retested for COVID-19 during the lead-up to the performance. Personal protective equipment was also necessary, with show producers securing 25,000 face masks to be used by all staff and performers.[8] During the performance itself, The Weeknd's dancers wore masks along with the bandages wrapped around their heads.

The Weeknd starred in several commercials for the brand that were shown during the game. One featured random people singing along to "Blinding Lights" while performing everyday activities, such as blow-drying their hair or stocking groceries in a supermarket. Another saw the singing star walking through the tunnels of Raymond James Stadium, appearing to psych himself up for his enormous performance to come.

The Super Bowl has become a place for artists to express themselves during their performances. Lady Gaga recited a portion of the Pledge of Allegiance during her halftime show in 2017 as an acknowledgment of unity among all races and genders. In 2020 Jennifer Lopez featured a cape with dual

Super Bowl halftime shows are often theatrical events with fireworks, but some performers also use the platform to convey social messages.

American and Puerto Rican flags as a nod to her Latina heritage. The Weeknd did not make any explicit political statements as part of his Super Bowl performance.

The Weeknd has become one of the top music acts of any genre in today's pop-culture landscape.

The Weeknd has come a long way from a relatively unknown suburb east of Toronto, Canada. The singer has made a monumental impact on music, beginning as a mysterious R&B performer who gave his music away for free on the internet and eventually transforming into an internationally recognized pop superstar who creates irresistible hooks for mainstream radio. Though The Weeknd had to make some changes to his work to appeal to mass-market audiences, he remains committed to his personal style, the emotions and messages he conveys with his music, and his unique brand of R&B artistry.

> "The Weeknd has earned this moment, and watching him smirking pridefully through entertaining an audience of millions was an incredible bookend to the borderline anonymity of the mixtape trilogy days (and maybe even a useful blueprint for a future residency somewhere in Las Vegas)."[9]
> —*Craig Jenkins*, Vulture

Chapter Two

FROM THE SUBURBS OF TORONTO

The international R&B sensation now known as The Weeknd came into the world in the middle of a long Canadian winter. Born Abel Tesfaye on February 16, 1990, he grew up in Scarborough, a suburb located east of Toronto, Ontario. His parents had immigrated to Canada from Ethiopia in the 1980s, joining the people of many other nationalities making up the population of the Greater Toronto Area.

Abel's parents split up when he was young, and he spent a lot of time with his grandmother because his mother had to work a lot. He was completely immersed in his family's culture at this time, speaking only the Ethiopian language of Amharic. These African roots would figure prominently in his development as a musical

The Toronto area was where The Weeknd grew up and began to craft his music career.

artist later in his life. He spent his downtime listening to Ethiopian artists such as Mulatu Astatke, Tilahun Gessesse, Mahmoud Ahmed, and Aster Aweke, musicians he would later credit as major influences. He was also a devoted fan of the internationally recognized King of Pop— Michael Jackson.

MASTERING MULTIPLE LANGUAGES

Languages were a constant source of frustration for Abel. He used Amharic at home because his grandmother would not speak English. He soon discovered that English was used by a great number of Canadians, and a majority of the television he watched was in that language, so he soon picked it up. But when he went to French-immersion school, he wasn't allowed

THE STARS OF SCARBOROUGH

Scarborough is one of Toronto's bigger suburbs. It has a population of more than 600,000 people. The multicultural threads of Toronto extend deep into Scarborough, with immigrants from China, the Philippines, and India forming just a few of the many largely foreign-born residential neighborhoods. The Weeknd is not the only famous person to come from Scarborough. Actor Mike Myers is also from the area, as is former NBA player Jamaal Magloire.

THE SEEDS OF INFLUENCE

Abel's mother tried to get him to take piano lessons when he was younger to cultivate his musical interest. He preferred pop music, but his tastes ranged across many genres. Rap and R&B were favorites, though he also went through a phase that included some giants of 1960s and 1970s rock. In junior high he began listening to the likes of Jimi Hendrix, Pink Floyd, and Led Zeppelin.

to speak English. Due to the constraints at both home and school, English became his third language.

Abel had a habit of singing in class, which constantly got him into trouble, both in school and with his mother. Abel's mom moved from job to job to support herself and

French is used widely in Canada, and it was one of the languages Abel grew up with.

her son. She fawned on Abel, but he remembered feeling lonely and wanting a sibling, preferably a brother, to keep him company when his mother was too busy. His father, Makkonen Tesfaye, was not present in his life. He gave Abel the middle name Makkonen. This is one of the few facts Abel knew about his father. Makkonen left the family in the earliest years of Abel's life, and despite occasional encounters with Abel at the ages of six and 12, he was not a paternal figure in the young boy's life.

MEETING THE MAN BEHIND *THE MASK*

The first movie Abel saw was *The Mask*. He was only four years old when his mother took him to a screening of the Jim Carrey comedy. The film made a huge impression on the youngster, and he became enamored with movies of all kinds. He had even hoped to attend film school, but he ultimately chose music as his art form because creating a song brought much quicker results than making a film. The Weeknd's relationship with *The Mask* came full circle when he became friends with Jim Carrey. The pair even ate breakfast together on The Weeknd's thirtieth birthday.

"I'm a mama's boy. Everything good, I get from my mother."[1]
–*The Weeknd*

BREAKING LOOSE AND MOVING DOWNTOWN

Abel bounced around to several schools, including West Hill Collegiate and Birchmount Park Collegiate, both

> "I got into a lot of trouble, got kicked out of school, moved to different schools and finally dropped out. I really thought film was gonna be my way out, but I couldn't really make a movie to feel better, you know? Music was very direct therapy; it was immediate and people liked it. It definitely saved my life."[2]
>
> —*The Weeknd*

located in Scarborough, before making the decision to drop out at the age of 17. He wound up renting a one-bedroom house with friends in Parkdale, a neighborhood west of downtown Toronto. The freedom to do whatever he wanted was irresistible.

Abel lived in the Parkdale neighborhood near Toronto at a time when he was struggling in his life.

Abel and his friends would stay up through the night, roam the city streets, and partake in drugs. The chaos continued when Abel and his friends were evicted from the house. For a brief period he found himself homeless. He later recalled telling girls that he loved them just to be able to sleep at their apartments.

Abel was motivated by music and had an urge to create. While he enjoyed many of the R&B artists of the 1990s, including the Neptunes and Aaliyah, he also was inspired by rap, and he particularly admired 50 Cent. Abel, along with his friend Jesse Dempster, formed a rap duo called Bulleez N Nerdz. Dempster soon pulled away from music after dealing with the death of a friend, leaving Abel to start seeking out other projects.

Abel soon met up with Jeremy Rose, a producer with an interest in R&B. Rose and Abel met by

MULATU ASTATKE

Famed Ethiopian musical artist Mulatu Astatke is sometimes called the father of Ethiopian jazz. In a 2017 interview with the *Huffington Post*, he was asked about the influence his work has had on one of the biggest stars in the world. He was pleased that The Weeknd had described him as an influence but admitted that he hadn't listened to the R&B star's music. "I am into Ethiopian jazz and [The Weeknd] is into something different," Astatke said.[3]

50 Cent was among the rappers Abel looked up to as his musical career was beginning.

chance due to mutual friends, and when Rose played a beat from a song he had been working on for some time, Abel began to freestyle. A partnership soon formed.

The two partied and wrote songs together. They called themselves The Weekend. After Rose and Abel split due to creative differences, Abel dropped the last "e" in the stage name. He did this to avoid confusion and conflict with an existing Canadian band called The Weekend. Abel developed a new project. It would be a mixtape of bleak, drug-fueled tracks named for the old Parkdale party house. He planned to call it *House of Balloons*.

SHY, MYSTERIOUS, AND INSECURE

The Weeknd is notorious for rarely giving interviews. He has admitted in the past that he is insecure about his intellect, which he largely blames on his decision to drop out of high school. In the earliest days of his career, he would refuse all media interviews because he was so self-conscious. He attempted to improve his vocabulary by doing crossword puzzles. Eventually he discovered that refusing interviews played in his favor, creating a mysterious image that fit well with his brooding music.

THREE LITTLE MIXTAPES

The first mixtape that would ultimately become *House of Balloons* was constructed in pieces. Producer Jeremy Rose and The Weeknd had collaborated on a trio of songs: "What You Need," "Loft Music," and "The Morning (The Original Version)." When they parted ways, the producer agreed to allow The Weeknd to take the songs, as long as Rose was given credit for his work when they were released.

In early 2011, The Weeknd uploaded the three tracks on YouTube under the username "xoxxxoooxo." The artist was listed as The Weeknd, but no other information was given. The Weeknd was self-conscious about his appearance, so he posted only photos and videos of himself in shadow. No one outside of The Weeknd's insular group knew the truth. People were unsure of the identity of "The Weeknd." Furthermore, they didn't know

The Weeknd's career began to take off in 2011.

27

STRUGGLING TO FIT THE IMAGE

When he first began, The Weeknd did not think he fit the mold of an R&B star. His appearance was a source of frustration for him. He felt he was not physically fit or attractive enough, and he generally felt awkward about himself. Not featuring himself in any of the early artwork for his mixtapes served a dual purpose. He could remain hidden from view while also fueling the mystery surrounding his music. In fact, he kept his identity so well hidden that while working a job at American Apparel, his coworkers would play his tapes without realizing that the voice coming from the speakers was in their presence.

whether the music had been made by a group or a single person.

Two weeks later, the independent entertainment site Pitchfork was wondering the same thing when staff writer Larry Fitzmaurice published a short review of the trio of tunes. Fitzmaurice gave the songs a glowing write-up. The buzz was growing. Adding fuel to the fire was superstar rapper Drake, also a native of Toronto. Drake had known about The Weeknd since 2009, when the two had first met. They crossed paths when The Weeknd contributed to a song called "Birthday Suit" that he hoped would land on Drake's first album. While the track didn't make the final cut, Drake always remembered The Weeknd and kept tabs on his career.

Drake was a key figure early in The Weeknd's career.

DRAKE BEGINS TO SPREAD THE WORD

Drake began tweeting out lyrical hints in the weeks leading up to the release of *House of Balloons*, quoting lines from the song "Wicked Games." When the *House of Balloons* mixtape was finally released in late March, critics praised it. The Weeknd's debut was a success. *House of Balloons* was short-listed for the Polaris Music Prize, a

Canadian musical award that is decided by a jury and comes with a $50,000 endowment.

The tape's artwork continued to play off The Weeknd's mystique, with the artist nowhere to be seen. Instead, the cover featured a partially nude woman shot in black-and-white and surrounded by balloons. In the midst of the hype over *House of Balloons*, The Weeknd prepared to bring his music to live audiences.

NATIONAL HONORS

Despite it being a free, self-released mixtape spread by word of mouth, *House of Balloons* made enough of an impact that the website of the Canadian Broadcasting Corporation referenced it six years after its release in a list of the 25 best Canadian album debuts. The list put The Weeknd's release in such company as Arcade Fire's *Funeral*, Leonard Cohen's *Songs of Leonard Cohen*, The Band's *Music from Big Pink*, and Avril Lavigne's *Let Go*.

THE FIRST SHOW

The Weeknd played his first show in July 2011 at a Toronto club. The elusiveness and secrecy continued even as he prepared for a live performance. Flyers explained that there would be no cameras and no media allowed. The only way to obtain a ticket was to purchase one directly from a downtown shoe store.

Drake and The Weeknd performed together at the OVO Music Festival in August 2013.

The show sold out quickly. Drake attended the show, watching from the balcony.

Drake was interested in collaborating with The Weeknd. He wanted the R&B singer to join his OVO Music Festival. Better still, Drake wanted The Weeknd to be involved in his next album, called *Take Care*. The Weeknd contributed to four songs on the album.

Drake's help would give him a boost, but The Weeknd wasn't done with his own projects. He released two more mixtapes before the end of 2011. *Thursday* dropped in August. Drake made an appearance on the song "The Zone." *Echoes of Silence*, which featured a cover of Michael Jackson's "Dirty Diana," released in December. The demand for the release was so high that the attempted

The Weeknd's cover of a song by pop megastar Michael Jackson, who had died just a few years earlier, was one of his early hits.

downloads crashed the servers of The Weeknd's website.

Like his other 2011 releases, *Echoes* was free for fans

to download.

Following the success of The Weeknd's mixtapes, he began to receive attention from the mainstream music industry. His career was about to reach new heights. And looking back on those early mixtapes, The Weeknd is well aware of the influence he has had on the music business. In a 2015 *Rolling Stone* interview, he told journalist Josh Eells, "A lot of artists started doing things faster and quicker after that: Justin Timberlake dropped two albums in a year, Beyoncé dropped a surprise album." He's equally proud of the music itself: "I'm not gonna say any names, but just listen to the radio. Every song is *House of Balloons 2.0.*"[1]

A NEW CHAPTER

In 2012 The Weeknd hit the road for his first appearances in the United States. He was invited to play Coachella, a major festival in Indio, California, that features many genres of music. The Weeknd played both Sundays of the two-weekend festival in April to kick off the beginning of his spring tour. While he did not play on the main stage, his presence and performance were positively reviewed by music publications such as *Billboard*. It was during the same month that he made his first appearance on the *Billboard* Hot 100 chart, when he was featured on Drake's song "Crew Love" from the album *Take Care*.

STARS IN THE CROWD

By June he was making his way overseas for shows in Europe. Spain, Belgium, France, and Portugal were on his schedule, as was the United Kingdom. The UK show in particular was notable for the well-known faces in the crowd. Pop superstar Katy Perry was spotted in the VIP section, as was Florence Welch of Florence + the Machine.

The Weeknd's performance at Coachella drew acclaim from both audiences and critics.

It was a small affair with just 300 people. But the size of the show definitely did not reflect the demand. The performance was sold out, and tickets that had been obtained for their face value of £20 were being scalped for £350.[1] As his tour continued into the fall through Canadian and American cities, The Weeknd was joined on his final dates by Welch and indie rock band the Maccabees.

In September, the Universal Republic label came calling, and he signed with it. Along with his own representation came the signing of a project called XO. This group was made up of The Weeknd and his friends Amir "Cash" Esmailian and Wassim "Sal" Slaiby. They created their own record label, XO Records, which would be

PRACTICE MAKES PERFECT

Performing at Coachella was a watershed moment in The Weeknd's career. It was his first US appearance, and he was doing it at a major music festival. He initially thought his appearances had gone well. But when he reviewed the recordings of the shows, his opinion dramatically changed. He described the experience as a "nightmare," and after reading some online comments about his show, he felt even worse.[2] He then buckled down, taking dance lessons and asking his agent to put him back out on the road so he could gain more confidence and experience as a performer.

distributed by Universal. The members of XO had worked together since the *House of Balloons* era, but the creation of their own record label allowed them to create on a much bigger scale. They would go on to work with artists such as Belly, M.I.A., and Daft Punk.

That same year, producer Jeremy Rose gave an explosive interview to *Vice*. He gave the backstory on his involvement in The Weeknd's early work. Rose was the one who approached The Weeknd about working on an R&B endeavor together, and they had collaborated on the tracks that gained momentum among media outlets such as Pitchfork and the *New York Times*. The two eventually had creative differences, and Rose chose

DISPUTES WITH DRAKE

In 2012 Drake was working on signing The Weeknd to his OVO label. The rapper told MTV that the deal was still in progress. But several months later, The Weeknd had a change of heart. He ultimately signed with Universal Republic. While Drake and The Weeknd had a working relationship on and off for the next few years, they continued to have issues with each other. In 2015 The Weeknd claimed he gave up half of his own album for Drake to use on Drake's *Take Care*, an accusation that Drake disputed. In 2017 rumors ran wild when tabloids speculated that Drake might be dating The Weeknd's former girlfriend, Bella Hadid. But by 2019 the situation between them seemed to be resolved when Drake addressed the end of the feud in the song "War."

to leave. However, when *House of Balloons* was released, all mention of Rose was removed, and he was not paid for his work. Rose eventually received a producer credit on a later release of the material.

Universal Republic gave The Weeknd's career a boost by repackaging his earlier releases for a new audience.

The Weeknd's 2012 tour included a November stop in his hometown, Toronto.

TRILOGY'S MUSIC VIDEOS

The singles from *Trilogy* came with accompanying videos. The video for "The Zone" was directed by The Weeknd and filmed in Montreal. The theme recalled imagery from the mixtapes, including bunches of balloons. The video for "Twenty Eight" is cloaked behind the age-restricted portion of YouTube. It features The Weeknd singing as the video cuts between portions of an interview with a gray-suited man and then shifts suddenly to a scene with topless dancers. "Wicked Games" is a black-and-white affair, with The Weeknd being filmed in alternating shadow and light. At one point, a dancer reaches out her hand and the silhouette of her fingers appears to brush across The Weeknd's face.

In November 2012, the label took the first three mixtapes, *House of Balloons*, *Thursday*, and *Echoes of Silence*, and put them out as a single package titled *Trilogy*. The collection also included three previously unreleased songs: "Valerie," "Till Dawn (Here Comes the Sun)," and "Twenty Eight," which became one of the album's singles. *Trilogy* debuted on the *Billboard* chart at Number 4. It peaked at Number 2 and would go on to spend 128 weeks on the charts. The record produced two other singles, "Wicked Games" and a collaboration with Drake called "The Zone."

WELCOME TO *KISS LAND*

The next year, 2013, marked the release of The Weeknd's first studio album. *Kiss Land* was released in September and debuted on the *Billboard* charts at Number 2. He considered this record to be a snapshot of the "second chapter" of his life. Whereas the mixtapes were based on his life in Toronto, *Kiss Land* was deeply influenced by his travels overseas and the rhythm he had developed while on the road. He wrote songs while flying on planes or riding on tour buses. He recorded in foreign studios. It was a completely new environment for him compared with recording the songs from *Trilogy*, an experience he had described as "claustrophobic" because of spending so much time in Toronto.[3]

BEG, BORROW, OR SAMPLE

During the initial releases of *House of Balloons*, *Thursday*, and *Echoes of Silence*, The Weeknd used samples from various artists without fear of legal trouble. However, releasing *Trilogy* on a major label meant he would need to get formal permissions to include the samples. He needed clearance from Beach House for "The Party & The After Party" and from Siouxsie and the Banshees for "Glass Table Girls." Not all the songs would remain in their original forms for *Trilogy*. He was unable to get permission to use Aaliyah's "Rock the Boat" for his song "What You Need."

Fans attended an album signing event for *Kiss Land* after a concert in September 2013.

Kiss Land took inspiration from various sources, and it was flavored in particular by 1970s and 1980s icons like Stevie Nicks and Genesis. Drums that sounded remarkably similar to those in the Portishead song "Machine Gun" appeared on "Belong to the World." The Weeknd went so far as to write a letter to Portishead's producers, telling them that *Kiss Land* had been inspired by the band. But when the video for the song appeared online, Portishead's Geoff Barrow blasted The Weeknd on Twitter, making the accusation that The Weeknd had used the sample without prior permission. Barrow tweeted, "When someone asks to sample you and you refuse they should have the respect as a fellow artist to not use it."[4] Barrow went on

Portishead is a prominent band in the trip-hop genre. This type of music mixes elements of hip-hop and electronic music.

to bolster his argument by posting a formal request sent to Portishead from The Weeknd, asking for permission to sample the song. The Weeknd's request was denied, but the drum sounds remained on his song. On July 17, 2014, Barrow tweeted, "Seems @theweeknd [has] said there is no sample used or enough likeness to Machine Gun to warrant any infringement . . . or credit."[5] The two parties appeared to reach a stalemate, and no legal action was pursued.

The Weeknd was expecting that *Kiss Land* would catapult him into superstardom, but the album was not the massive smash hit he had expected. Reviews for *Kiss Land* were decidedly mixed. Pitchfork's Ian Cohen felt the record was missing the strong melodies from *House of Balloons*. He criticized The Weeknd's words, referring to his lyrics

THE INFLUENCE OF TRAVEL AND FILM

Part of the inspiration for *Kiss Land* came from The Weeknd's travels on his first major tour. He felt a great deal of fear and unfamiliarity being so far away from home. He was inspired by filmmakers such as John Carpenter, David Cronenberg, and Ridley Scott because he admired their ability to capture the emotion of fear. He wanted to create a landscape of horror within *Kiss Land* to accurately portray his feelings at the time.

as "often embarrassing, occasionally nonsensical and not worth quoting at length."[6] Chris Payne from *Billboard* appreciated the range of The Weeknd's voice, even when he was singing about troublesome topics: "Here, the Weeknd sets out to see what he can do with his voice. [The beat in] 'Adaptation' . . . builds momentum as it powers on, but Tesfaye's acrobatic leaps, from register to register, are the main selling point. He's singing about alcoholic models up all night, drinking away sadness, covering virtually all of his usual lyrical tropes in one fell swoop."[7]

After the album's release, The Weeknd briefly mulled over the idea of moving to Seattle, Washington. He thought the moody, rainy weather might kick-start his creativity. Ultimately, he made the decision to move to Los Angeles, California, a global center for the entertainment industry but also a place with a history of crushing dreams.

"No matter how dark my experiences were during *Trilogy*, it's nothing like L.A. L.A. is *dark*."[8]
–The Weeknd to Josh Eells, Rolling Stone

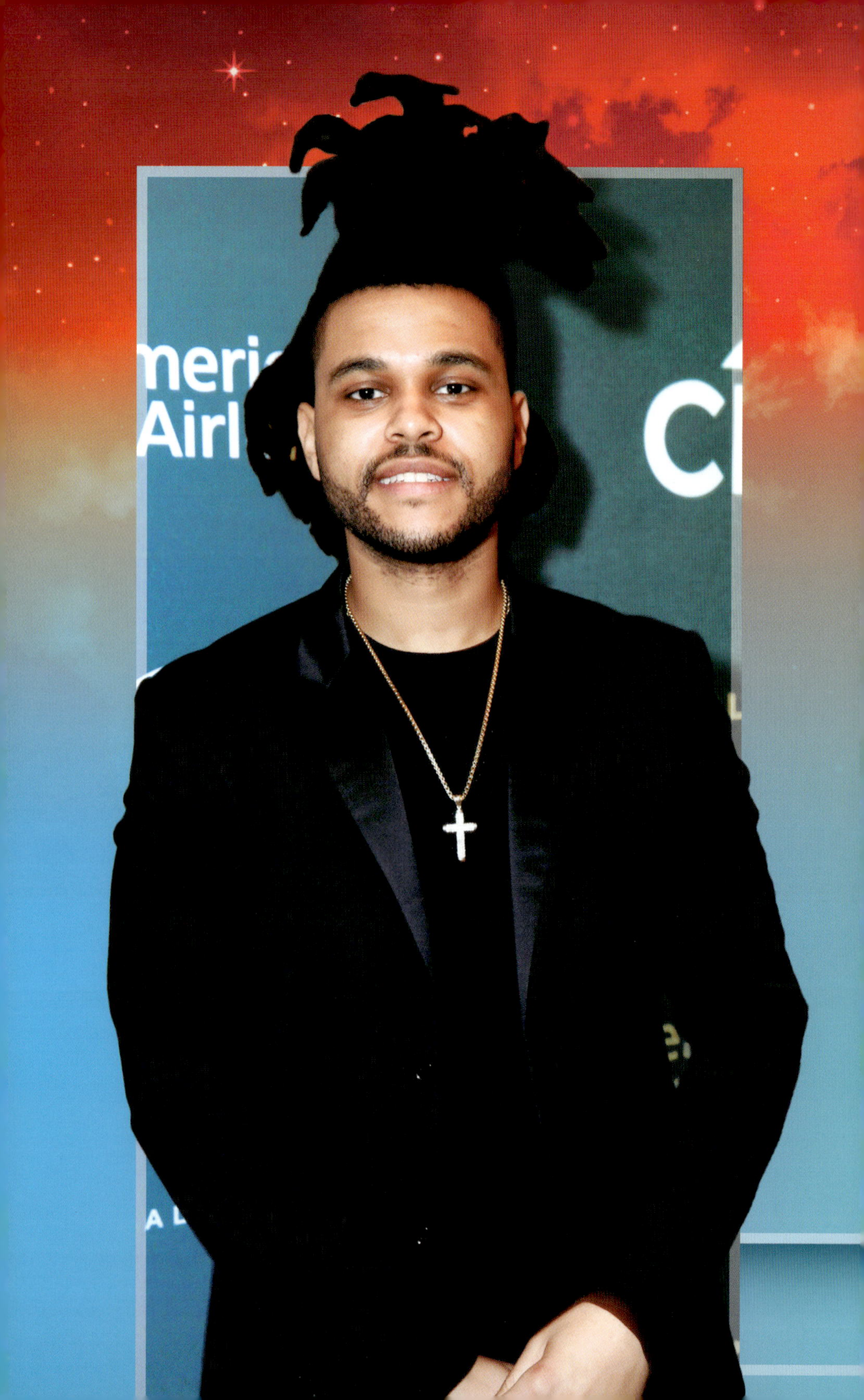

BLOWING UP

For The Weeknd, 2014 marked the beginning of an emergence into the wider world of mainstream pop music. This journey began with two songs: "Love Me Harder" and "Earned It." His shortcomings with *Kiss Land* had left him disheartened. He sought out the advice of a representative from his label, who asked The Weeknd whether he wanted to be the biggest star in the world. His answer was a resounding "yes." The rep put The Weeknd in contact with pop singer Ariana Grande.

Grande provided him with the song "Love Me Harder." When it arrived at The Weeknd's door, he was less than enthused. He felt the track was too tame for him, and he honestly wasn't sure whether his style would mesh with Grande's shiny pop image. But he wasn't completely dissuaded, so he went ahead with a verse rewrite and fired it back to her. Magic sparked. "Love Me Harder" was The Weeknd's first collaboration with Ariana Grande, and it became a single from her August 2014 album *My Everything*. The duet marked The Weeknd's first time in the

As The Weeknd's career grew, he continued to get involved with more high-profile collaborators, projects, and events.

The Weeknd and Ariana Grande performed their duet together at the American Music Awards in November 2014.

Top 10 of the *Billboard* Hot 100 List, peaking at Number 7 in November 2014. The music video has a cinematic vibe, complete with wide shots and moody lighting. It features the duo singing separately indoors while a vicious storm rages outside. When they appear together late in the video, they are standing back-to-back, backlit and stoic.

At the end of 2014, The Weeknd released "Earned It." The song was going to be a part of his next album, which was due in 2015. But it was also meant for the soundtrack for the film *Fifty Shades of Grey*. The movie was a hotly anticipated adaptation of the widely successful novel by E. L. James. The song was a departure from The Weeknd's usually brooding work. It is highly orchestral, featuring lush strings and piano, and is presented in waltz time. But The Weeknd's sultry, slow style is still evident in the tone and lyrics. The track hit Number 3 on the *Billboard* Hot 100 and earned The Weeknd an Oscar nomination in January 2016 for Best Original Song, along with cowriters Ahmad Balshe, Stephan Moccio, and Jason Quenneville.

When composer Stephan Moccio had been invited to work with The Weeknd, he knew it was rare to click with another artist right off the bat. Moccio was used to working with adult-contemporary superstars such as Celine Dion and Josh Groban.

> "Well, the thing is with Abel and his voice [and the way he is], he's just instantly seductive. And it's a sort of gentle seduction that just pulls you and pulls you and pulls you in, and for this movie it couldn't be more perfect."[1]
> —Sam Taylor-Johnson, director of Fifty Shades of Grey

He soon discovered that The Weeknd knew exactly what he wanted artistically. The composer's experience had taught him that if a singer is solely interested in record sales, the creative spark won't light. "If the artist is in more pursuit of fame, I typically am not as interested," Moccio told *Entertainment Tonight*. He added that The Weeknd's

Moccio, *left*, and The Weeknd attended an event celebrating the music of *Fifty Shades of Grey*.

reclusive vibe was his biggest selling point. "He's a very enigmatic kind of guy."[2]

BROADENING THE WEEKND'S APPEAL

"Love Me Harder" and "Earned It" exposed The Weeknd to new audiences. Fans of Ariana Grande largely resided in the pop vein, and moviegoers interested in *Fifty Shades of Grey* tended to be women who were more curious about James's newest novels than about R&B mixtapes. This wider interest in the singer came with many questions. However, they were not necessarily always about his music. People wanted to know about The Weeknd's hair.

A quick internet search of "The Weeknd hair" will return millions of results. Various websites have devoted articles to the evolution of his hairstyle. In a *Rolling Stone* interview

HAIR TODAY, GONE TOMORROW

Social media collectively exploded when it was revealed that The Weeknd had chopped off his famous hair in September 2016. The internet was flooded with photos of the new hairdo, a short style that was far tamer than his previous look. He later revealed that the cut gave him more freedom—he was sleeping better without interference, and he could finally wear a ballcap, affording him anonymity he previously lacked. However, the hair was not lost forever. The Weeknd's manager locked up the dreadlocks in a private safe.

The Weeknd's signature hairstyle became one of his trademarks.

from 2015 he said that his hair was somewhat inspired by the hairstyle of American graffiti artist Jean-Michel Basquiat. The Weeknd's hair in front was flopped over into bunches and locks. The sides were shaved, and the back was separated into several larger pieces, giving the overall look a sculptural effect.

GETTING BIG

In the spring of 2015, The Weeknd returned to Coachella for a triumphant performance. Gone was the anxious new artist; now The Weeknd was given the chance to close out the Saturday main stage. His voice was in top form, rising high above the din of the crowd. He moved through several of his well-known songs, including "Earned It." He performed a cover of Beyoncé's "Drunk in Love." It was a massive change from his Coachella shows from three years prior, when he was performing to only a few hundred people. "This is the greatest night of my entire life," The Weeknd told the crowd. "Nothing's better than right now."[3]

On August 28, 2015, The Weeknd released his second studio album, *Beauty behind the Madness*. The album debuted at Number 1 on the *Billboard* charts. *Beauty* became the most streamed album on Spotify in the music service's history. Between December 1, 2014, and December 1, 2015, the record was heard by 60 million listeners. The single "Can't Feel My Face" was streamed

PHOTOS FROM THE ROAD

The Weeknd's The Madness tour accompanied the release of *Beauty behind the Madness*. The Weeknd was joined by Travis Scott, Banks, and Halsey, giving the tour a mix of musical genres for fans to experience. Photographer Elie "Visionelie" Jonathan captured life on the road during the tour for the music magazine *Fader*. While there are plenty of shots of the shows themselves, other images record day-to-day happenings behind the scenes—The Weeknd playing video games with Scott, managers slicing into a birthday cake shaped like a car, and the performers walking the arena hallways prior to going onstage.

The Weeknd's 2015 Coachella performance was much larger in scale than his appearance at the same festival just a few years earlier.

448,334,867 times by January 13, 2016.[4] "Face" would become a Number 1 single, as would "The Hills." *Beauty behind the Madness* earned seven Grammy nominations, and The Weeknd won for Best R&B Performance, as well as Best Urban Contemporary Album.

In adjusting to mainstream tastes and expanding his listenership, The Weeknd brought pop elements into his sound. However, his style still had some harder edges, thanks to the frequent mentions of drug use in his songs. Publications such as *Billboard* have compiled articles devoted to listing the artist's drug references in his lyrics. Whether describing the drugs themselves or the feelings he experiences while on them, The Weeknd has made no secret of his drug use, both in his music and in the rare interviews he has given over the years.

The frequent drug references are accompanied by another one of The Weeknd's favorite topics: women. His derogatory mentions of women in his songs have led to questions and criticism. For his part, The Weeknd has insisted that he is playing "a character" while singing his lyrics and that he has never meant any offense with his words.[5]

"It was tempting to view *Beauty behind the Madness* as a cynical appeal to radio listeners but, in fact, the album represented a massive risk. *Beauty behind the Madness* is the result of The Weeknd and his collaborators heedfully seeking that sweet spot between engaging Top 40 and exquisite, R-rated urban pop."[6]
—*Bruce Britt*, Medium

Some critics applauded *Beauty behind the Madness*, calling it a successful sophomore effort after the slightly disappointing *Kiss Land.* Pitchfork reviewer Andrew Ryce noticed the slight turn The Weeknd's trajectory had taken toward the mainstream. However, he couldn't contain his amusement at the knowledge that pop kingmaker Max Martin had cowritten "Can't Feel My Face," a song about cocaine use. Ryce quipped that the tune was a "Weeknd song that's fun for the whole family."[7]

The Weeknd's involvement with "Love Me Harder" was also his introduction to Martin. The Swedish producer has worked with the likes of Katy Perry on "Roar" and Britney Spears on ". . . Baby One More Time." The Weeknd wanted Martin's help in smoothing out some of his rougher edges to make him more palatable for the mainstream market. It wasn't the easiest working relationship at first, and the two often found themselves at odds. But they eventually found their rhythm, and The Weeknd later referred to Martin as a close friend.

Jon Dolan of *Rolling Stone* caught on immediately to The Weeknd's fondness for Michael Jackson, specifically

Max Martin has worked with artists including Taylor Swift, the Backstreet Boys, and Katy Perry.

referencing two of Jackson's biggest works, *Thriller* and *Bad*, in his review of *Beauty behind the Madness*. But he also caught references to other acts of the 1980s, from singer-songwriter Tracy Chapman to power-pop superstar Phil Collins. While taking note of The Weeknd's growing appeal, he still lamented the underlying sadness, which he described as The Weeknd's "serious Eeyore vibe," throughout much of the album.[8]

DARKNESS REIGNS ON "IN THE NIGHT"

The concept for the song "In the Night," which appears on *Beauty behind the Madness*, was inspired by a couple of different historical references. Max Martin's studio was the former home of film star Marilyn Monroe. Monroe, who died in 1962, was an iconic actress and model who was one of the top Hollywood stars of the 1950s. The Weeknd came up with the idea of the song while spending time in Monroe's old bedroom. He thought of notorious beats like those featured in Michael Jackson's "The Way You Make Me Feel," and he wanted to use something similar. His producers were also listening to "Copacabana" by Barry Manilow and noted how the happy melody was juxtaposed with melancholy lyrics. The group took this influence to create a song with the same flavor.

Chapter SIX

LIVING IN THE SPOTLIGHT

The Weeknd began hinting at his next album in March 2016. On a Twitter post featuring a photo with the singer nearly enveloped in thick, oppressive smoke, he simply included the caption "Chapter done soon. Just let these pages flip." He had referred to his earlier albums as "chapters" of his life, so the post was a strong indication of something new in the works.[1]

SAYING NO TO RIHANNA

The creation of the new album was challenging. Early on in 2016, The Weeknd made the decision to pull out of a major summer tour with Rihanna. He wanted to have time to intensify his focus on songwriting. However, the choice led to pressure and stress that made it hard to work, which he ultimately blamed on the financial shortcomings

The Weeknd performed at the Grammy Awards in February 2016.

caused by the missed tour. To compensate for his writer's block, he returned to his old vices of alcohol and drugs.

The Weeknd thought back to old childhood favorites like the Wu-Tang Clan and 50 Cent to influence the album. He intended for the songs to have a grandstanding aspect, in line with the braggart style heard in some hip-hop. His ultimate goal was for the record to be contentious but seductive. He delved deep into a 1980s musical grab bag and came up with a wide variety of inspirations. The final product included references to British rock band the Smiths, punk stalwarts Bad Brains, the post-punk group Talking Heads, R&B group DeBarge, and rock icon Prince. The Weeknd also dabbled in the new wave and Britpop genres. The song "Secrets" contained samples from the Romantics' "Talking in Your Sleep" as well as "Pale Shelter" by Tears for Fears.

"It has not been revealed what has caused the dramatic change of plans, but The Weeknd did share a cryptic message on his Twitter page yesterday, as he wrote, 'it's my job to make music . . . not to convince you.'"[2]

—Edward Roberts, the Mirror, on The Weeknd pulling out of the tour with Rihanna

The Weeknd's next album would feature major 1980s influences, including nods to the music of American new wave band the Romantics.

SHOOTING FOR STRATOSPHERIC HEIGHTS: *STARBOY*

Starboy, The Weeknd's third full-length album, dropped on November 25, 2016. The record debuted at Number 1 on the *Billboard* 200 chart. *Starboy* included contributions from electronica duo Daft Punk, rapper

Kendrick Lamar, and singer-songwriter Lana Del Rey. In addition to hitting Number 1, The Weeknd achieved the remarkable feat of having every one of the album's

The Weeknd's *Starboy* tour brought him to huge venues, including American Airlines Arena in Miami, Florida.

18 songs appear simultaneously on the *Billboard* Hot 100. His accomplishment was second only to Drake's. The Weeknd's fellow Toronto native claimed 20 songs on the Hot 100 in May 2016, thanks to his album *Views*.

The album was generally well received by reviewers. Annie Zaleski of the pop-culture website the AV Club wrote, "[The Weeknd would] rather express everything he's feeling than put forth an airbrushed or idealized version of himself. In that sense, *Starboy* is one of the most confident releases of the year, one bold enough to reveal the cracks in The Weeknd's façade for the sake of resonant art."[3] Frank Guan of *Vulture* pointed out that The Weeknd jumped around to many genres throughout the record with ease, finding references to "rap, R&B, disco, electronic, electroclash, pop, and '80s pop."[4] But not everyone raved over the album. *Rolling Stone* expressed disappointment, giving *Starboy* three out of five

STARBOY SINGLES

Starboy produced multiple singles during its release. The title track and "I Feel It Coming" were dropped as singles, with the former hitting Number 1 on the *Billboard* Hot 100 chart. It was The Weeknd's third time atop the singles charts. He had previously hit the mark with "Can't Feel My Face" and "The Hills," both from *Beauty behind the Madness*.

stars. Reviewer Mosi Reeves lamented that the album sounded like "clichés wrapped in prettier packaging."[5] Allan Raible of ABC News mentioned that The Weeknd's voice had been overproduced with unnecessary effects and said that the entire album lacked his previous intrigue.

THE WEEKND AND DAFT PUNK TAKE THE STAGE

The Grammys took notice of *Starboy*. In 2017 The Weeknd took home the award for Best Urban Contemporary Album, his second victory in the category. He had previously won the same award for *Beauty behind the Madness* in 2015. The Weeknd and the duo Daft Punk came together for a live performance of "I Feel It Coming" and "Starboy" at the awards show. The Grammys stage was bathed in purple and blue light as the three performed together, The Weeknd dressed casually while the two members of Daft Punk wore black robes and polished black helmets.

HAPPINESS FOLLOWED BY HURT

Following the release of *Starboy*, The Weeknd's personal life would play a compelling role in his next release. He began dating pop star Selena Gomez at the beginning of 2017. The two had a whirlwind romance, which included chic holidays to Italy, yacht rides along the California coast, and many public displays of affection recorded by the paparazzi. But by October, the two had broken up. Some said it was due to too much time spent apart.

By 2018 The Weeknd was ready to release his next project. *My Dear Melancholy* came out on March 30. The mournful six-song extended play (EP) recalled some of his earlier work from the *House of Balloons* era. The brooding tone combined with the timing of the drop led many to believe that the album was the emotional fallout of The Weeknd's breakup with Gomez.

Whereas *Starboy* may have felt too slick for some reviewers, *My Dear Melancholy* was jarring and emotional. Tirhakah Love of *Rolling Stone* wrote, "Perhaps contrary to his

WHAT COULD HAVE BEEN

Prior to dropping *My Dear Melancholy*, The Weeknd had completed a totally separate album with a flavor that contrasted sharply with the 2018 release. He described the unreleased project as "upbeat" and "very beautiful" because it had been written during his time with Gomez.[6] He made the decision to do away with the record, because he felt that portion of his life was over. The Weeknd said that after the breakup, writing *Melancholy* was a restorative experience for him, allowing him to shut the door on an unpleasant chapter in his life.

"It's therapeutic. You want to get it out. It's like you close a chapter."[7]
—The Weeknd on creating My Dear Melancholy

posture on previous albums, where he presented his unfeeling lust as a kind of immature frivolity, *My Dear Melancholy* interestingly connects his sex and substance use to the pain of romantic sacrifice."[8]

ABEL AND BELLA

As an R&B artist known for performing sultry songs, The Weeknd and his romantic life have long been fodder for the tabloids. The Weeknd's longest relationship of note was with supermodel Bella Hadid. The two began dating in 2015. Hadid would appear in The Weeknd's video for "In the Night." The duo kept the tabloids on their toes, breaking up and reconciling multiple times over the course of four years before seemingly splitting for good in 2019.

WORKING WITH EVERYONE

The Weeknd has been a collaborator since the earliest days of his career. Dating back to 2011, when he contributed songs toward Drake's second album, *Take Care*, he has actively worked on other artists' projects. He has also included others in his own releases. These shared undertakings were particularly beneficial early in The Weeknd's career. Working with larger stars, such as Drake and Ariana Grande, provided additional exposure for his music.

The Weeknd's partnership on "Dark Times" with singer-songwriter Ed Sheeran began at a June 2015 party. Sheeran was in Toronto to host the Much Music Video Awards when he received an invitation to come over to The Weeknd's condo. Sheeran was initially hesitant because he thought the R&B artist wouldn't want to work with him. He knew that Kanye West was already involved

The Weeknd frequently works with other artists, including English star Ed Sheeran.

One of The Weeknd's most consistent collaborators is rapper Travis Scott. Scott first had The Weeknd appear on his 2015 album, *Rodeo*, performing on the song "Pray for Love." That same year, Scott opened for The Weeknd on tour, and the two performed Scott's song "Wonderful" together. That track went on to be a single in 2016. Scott featured The Weeknd on his 2018 album *Astroworld* on the tracks "Skeletons" and "Wake Up." And in 2019, the two contributed "Power Is Power" to an album of songs inspired by *Game of Thrones*. The song is heavy with references to the fantasy television show, and it also includes singer-songwriter SZA.

in The Weeknd's album and assumed that the rap mogul was going to be the focus of any collaborative efforts. What began as a long night of partying turned into songwriting the next day. Kanye was a part of *Beauty behind the Madness*, producing the track "Tell Your Friends," but Sheeran made the cut too.

Another collaborator from *Beauty behind the Madness* was pop singer Lana Del Rey, who joined The Weeknd on "Prisoner." Del Rey creates a dark, cinematic vibe with her music, making her a logical fit alongside The Weeknd's gloomy musical persona. The Weeknd has described her as being an inspiration for his music, and the two have worked together on multiple songs, including the title track on Del Rey's *Lust for Life* album.

Lana Del Rey has been one of The Weeknd's frequent collaborators.

THE WEEKND TACKLES A FOURTH LANGUAGE

One of The Weeknd's most intriguing partnerships happened in late 2020. Colombian singer Maluma had a smash hit in August of that year with the reggaeton song "Hawái." The track rocketed up *Billboard*'s charts, becoming

THE WEEKND TAKES ON QUEEN BEY

One of The Weeknd's most notable collaborations came in 2016. Pop superstar Beyoncé included The Weeknd on "6 Inch" as both a cowriter and featured artist. The album featuring the song, *Lemonade*, made waves as both a musical and a cultural phenomenon that included commentary on feminism and racism.

FRIENDS AND COLLABORATORS

Electronica music mainstays Daft Punk have been a major inspiration for The Weeknd, and he got to work with the famous duo on his *Starboy* album. The Weeknd was so enamored with Daft Punk that initially he was just looking for a way to get better acquainted with the two. Four days of work in a Paris studio resulted in two songs: "I Feel It Coming" and the album's title track, "Starboy." In a single day, "Starboy" racked up a record-breaking 40 million streams on Spotify.[1]

one of the hottest songs of the summer. Other artists had shown interest in doing a remix, but Maluma initially wasn't interested. He hadn't ever remixed any of his songs in other languages, and he didn't want to change "Hawái." There was, however, the chance that if someone notable wanted to work on a remix with him, he might be interested.

Maluma and The Weeknd were excited to work together, and their remix turned out to be a major hit.

It was a very short list of people, and The Weeknd was on it. Luckily for Maluma, The Weeknd was a massive fan of the song and was excited to contribute. They began hammering out vocals via a group chat. The final product features The Weeknd singing in English, and for the first time, Spanish. The collaboration earned Maluma his first Hot 100 Top 10 hit, when the remix peaked at Number 4 in December 2020.

The Weeknd surprised fans with yet another Spanish remix in 2020. This time the collaboration involved one of his own songs. Not long after the one-year anniversary release of "After Hours," The Weeknd dropped a remix of the song with Spanish superstar singer Rosalía. This bilingual duet features Rosalía beginning the song in Spanish, with The Weeknd joining her in English for the chorus.

BREAKING DOWN THE BEST DUETS

Given The Weeknd's penchant for working with others both on remixes and original songs, many lists have appeared online discussing his most popular collaborations. *Entertainment Weekly* rated "Crew Love" with Drake at Number 3 and "I Feel It Coming" with Daft Punk at Number 4 in its ranking of singles on which The Weeknd performs. In fact, 24 of 45 songs in the website's list feature The Weeknd collaborating with another artist, including performers such as Sia, Ty Dolla $ign, Wiz Khalifa, DJ Khaled, Future, and Kendrick Lamar.[2]

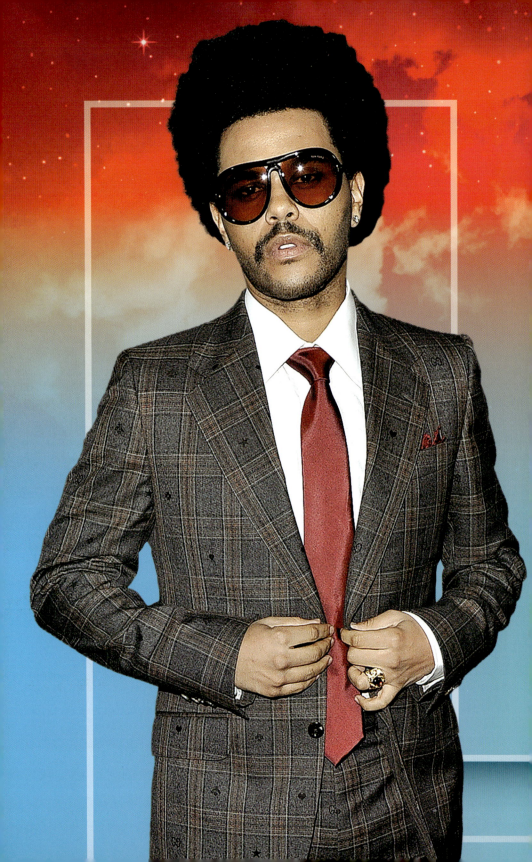

AFTER HOURS AND BEYOND

The Weeknd again became involved in controversy regarding his lyrics in 2019, but this time it came via a collaboration. The Weeknd worked with French DJ Gesaffelstein on the song "Lost in the Fire." The track was initially seen as a diss track directed at Drake, who was rumored to have dated The Weeknd's on-and-off love interest Bella Hadid. But some listeners took to Twitter to call out lyrics they described as blatantly misogynistic and offensive toward bisexual people. In the song, The Weeknd implies that he can change a woman's sexual preference by having sex with her, and he also refers to being a lesbian as "a phase."[1] Karlie Powell of the website Your EDM suggested that while The Weeknd's lyrics have always been sexualized and graphic, he may have taken this one too far.

In 2019 and 2020, The Weeknd attracted controversy, weathered the COVID-19 pandemic, and took his career to new heights of success.

Late that year, The Weeknd began teasing his next major project. On November 26, 2019, he tweeted, "TONIGHT WE START A BRAIN MELTING PSYCHOTIC CHAPTER LET'S GOOOO."[2] *After Hours* was released on March 20, 2020. The Weeknd's fourth full-length studio album came into the world right as the COVID-19 pandemic began impacting the daily lives of people around the world. He managed to get in just a few appearances to support the album, including a turn on *Saturday Night Live*, before restrictions on crowds made live events impossible.

The restrictions stemming from the COVID-19 pandemic left live performance venues around the world empty for many months.

Despite not being able to go out and properly perform for his fans, The Weeknd still managed to keep people talking. He created a persona he referred to as "The Character" in interviews. "The Character" regularly sported a red suit jacket, a black shirt, and black trousers. The story of "The Character" began in the video for "Heartless" and flowed through subsequent videos for "Blinding Lights," "After Hours," "In Your Eyes," and "Until I Bleed Out." His progression was meant to reflect a life of bizarre behavior and danger.

Throughout these videos, The Weeknd appears in different stages of injury. He first sports a nose bandage, then eventually turns up with his head completely swathed in medical gauze. In the video for "Save Your Tears," his face has undergone a frightening transformation, seemingly the victim of an overzealous plastic surgeon. He stares down the camera with an ultrasmooth forehead and gigantic, plumped cheeks. When asked about the significance of the bandages in an interview with *Variety*, The Weeknd said it was a commentary on the nature of celebrity and the extreme measures to which many will subject themselves for the purposes of obtaining approval and acceptance.

The Weeknd collected an award at the American Music Awards in November 2020 wearing his "The Character" outfit.

UNPACKING *AFTER HOURS*

The Weeknd used a song on *After Hours* to touch on an ugly incident from five years prior. Early in the morning of January 10, 2015, The Weeknd was arrested for punching a police officer in Las Vegas. He was charged with one count of misdemeanor battery of a protected person. He pleaded no contest and was required to complete an anger management course, undergo alcohol evaluation, and perform 50 hours of community service. He also paid a $1,000 fine, which was given to a police fund created to benefit injured officers. The *After Hours* song "Faith" closes with police sirens as an acknowledgment of the arrest.

On *After Hours*, The Weeknd's passion for movies appeared once again as an influence. He drew on Martin Scorsese's 1985 film *After Hours,* Terry Gilliam's take on the Hunter S. Thompson novel *Fear and Loathing in Las Vegas*, and Roman Polanski's *Chinatown,* among others. All of these movies have a running theme of excess and trickery.

After Hours proved to be another massive commercial success for the star. The album debuted at Number 1 on the *Billboard* 200 chart. By March 30, 2020, all 14 of the record's tracks were on the *Billboard* Hot 100. The Number 1 hit "Blinding Lights" set a *Billboard* record, becoming the first song to spend a full 52 weeks in the Top 10.

BOYCOTTING THE GRAMMYS

In 2021 The Weeknd made international news when he announced his decision to boycott the Grammys. *After Hours* would have been eligible for the 2021 Grammys. The record received accolades from reviewers and was included on many critics' "Best of the Year" playlists. When the nominations for the awards were announced,

> "If you were like, 'Do you think the Grammys are racist?' I think the only real answer is that in the last 61 years of the Grammys, only 10 Black artists have won album of the year. I don't want to make this about me. That's just a fact."[3]
> —*The Weeknd to Katie Bain*, Billboard

The Weeknd was completely shut out. He blamed the committees responsible for making the final decision on the nominations.

In a statement to the *New York Times*, The Weeknd made his feelings plain: "Because of the secret committees, I will no longer

The Weeknd has been recognized with a number of awards over the years, but in 2021 he decided to no longer put himself up for Grammy Awards.

allow my label to submit my music to the Grammys."[4] Several other high-profile Black artists, including Drake, Frank Ocean, and Kanye West, have also turned their backs on the Grammys, as they feel the awards do not accurately represent, celebrate, or acknowledge musical artists of color.

As a confirmed superstar, The Weeknd's bank account grew to match his fame. In 2017 he earned $92 million, which put him at Number 6 on *Forbes*'s list of the top 100 highest earning celebrities, and he was featured on the cover of the magazine.[5] In 2020 he was estimated to be worth more than $100 million. The Weeknd also dabbled in some expensive real estate. He had come a long way from the small *House of*

WHAT GRAMMYS?

The Weeknd may have been snubbed by the Grammys in 2021, but other musical institutions were prepared to heap plenty of nominations on him for *After Hours*. At the end of April, *Billboard* announced that The Weeknd was nominated for 16 of its awards, including top male artist, top R&B artist, top *Billboard* 200 album, and top Hot 100 song for "Blinding Lights." He was also the most nominated artist in his home country of Canada for the 2021 Junos. The Junos are an annual award ceremony celebrating Canadian artists. The Weeknd was included on six lists, including fan choice, single of the year, album of the year, artist of the year, songwriter of the year, and contemporary R&B recording of the year.

Balloons house in Toronto. While with Bella Hadid, The Weeknd rented a New York penthouse for $60,000 per month.

However, a mansion in Hidden Hills, California, north of Los Angeles, may be the most famous of his residences. The Weeknd paid $18.2 million for the home, which sprawls over 13,500 square feet and sits on three acres of land.[6] The residence includes a basketball court with the three-point lines painted in bright orange. The garage floor is covered in mirrors and includes neon lights that can change between blue, purple, and green. The flashy space was used to show off The Weeknd's car collection. In 2020 he was the owner of a Lamborghini Aventador SV roadster, an old-school Porsche 911 from the

1980s, a Bentley Mulsanne, and a McLaren P1 hypercar. Despite the mansion's amenities, The Weeknd kept the house for only three years before selling it in 2021 to another musical superstar—Madonna.

After the mansion, The Weeknd decided to downsize somewhat, though not necessarily in price. He spent a whopping $21 million on a penthouse apartment in the middle of Los Angeles. His newest pad measured 8,200 square feet (760 sq m).[7] It featured high ceilings, two balconies, four bedrooms, a gym, and around-the-clock security.

The McLaren P1 starts at a price of more than $1 million.

In May 2021 The Weeknd marked a notable accomplishment on the *Billboard* charts. He had three simultaneous Number 1 hits on three of *Billboard*'s charts. His "Save Your Tears" remix with Ariana Grande topped both the Pop Airplay and Adult Pop charts. Meanwhile, the monster hit "Blinding Lights" dominated the Adult Contemporary listings. By May 14, the song had reigned over the chart for an astounding 24 weeks.

The "Save Your Tears" remix helped The Weeknd achieve yet another unusual milestone. When the song hit Number 1 on the *Billboard* charts, it helped the *After Hours* album match an achievement previously reached only by pop diva Janet Jackson. Both The Weeknd's album and Jackson's *Janet Jackson's Rhythm Nation 1814* had Number 1 singles land on the charts in three different years. The Weeknd's "Heartless" went to Number 1 at the end of 2019. "Blinding Lights" was released in the same week, but it took much longer to climb up the charts. It finally topped the list in April 2020. "Save Your Tears" made it to Number 1 on May 3, 2021, following the release of the remixed version of the track featuring Ariana Grande.

The Weeknd kept the momentum of the "Save Your Tears" remix going, beaming in remotely to make an appearance at the 2021 Brit Awards. He donned a rain jacket and hat while performing the song in a stark, three-walled room. As the camera panned out, viewers could see that he was not alone. It wasn't Ariana Grande, but Oneohtrix Point Never—who collaborated with The Weeknd on *After Hours*—providing melodies from the opposite corner. As the song reached its climax, rain began to pour down outside of the room.

The Weeknd appeared at the Billboard Music Awards in May 2021.

THE MOMENTUM CONTINUES

Songs from *After Hours* continued to receive a great deal of airplay in the spring of 2021, but The Weeknd had already begun to think about his next record. In an interview with *Variety*, he was asked about what might be in the works. He told Jem Aswad, "If the last record is the after hours of the night, then the dawn is coming." Just a few days prior to the interview's release, The Weeknd tweeted several times about what might be going on behind the scenes. "Made so much magic in the small quarantined room," he tweeted on April 27, 2021. "Now just piecing it all together . . . it's so beautiful."[1]

In the spring of 2021, the Recording Academy, the organization behind the Grammy Awards, made a significant announcement. It declared that it would no longer be using secret committees to review and determine nominations. The Weeknd believed these

Throughout his career, The Weeknd has always been looking ahead to new creative directions.

"I have been more inspired and creative during the pandemic than I might normally be while out on the road. The pandemic, the Black Lives Matter Movement and the tensions of the election have mostly created a sense of gratitude for what I have and a closeness with the people near me."[3]

–The Weeknd to journalist Malik Peay

MAINTAINING FOCUS

Despite ten years passing since the release of his first mixtape, The Weeknd insists that his work ethic has not changed. He claims to be as "laser focused" in those early years as he is today. He told Glenn Rowley of *Billboard* magazine, "I feel like I spent the last 10 years creating a sound and most of my career, I've either been running away from it or duplicating it. *After Hours* was the perfect piece of art for me to show my tenure in the industry."[4]

groups had played a large part in keeping him out of the Grammy selection process for *After Hours*. The Weeknd acknowledged the announcement as a step in the right direction, but he also insisted that the Academy's admission of guilt and "corruption" prompted him to stand firm on his decision not to submit his music for Grammy consideration going forward.[2]

MAKING HIS MARK

The Weeknd has made a major impact on the world of pop and R&B music. The initial decision to make his first three mixtapes free to anyone gave him direct access to his audience.

Marketing, media spin, and record label sales pitches did not get between him and his early fans. He was in complete control of not only his music but also his image, choosing to remain largely anonymous in the early years.

House of Balloons, *Thursday*, and *Echoes of Silence* were distinct from the work of R&B crooners from decades past. The Weeknd presented sets of contrasting themes, disinterested yet agitated, filled with desire but also self-loathing. He pushed the notion of isolation amid decadent partying, making the idea seem almost sensual while at the same time reminding his listeners that this world was an unpleasant place to be. It was not long before echoes of The Weeknd's sound could be heard among his colleagues in the music business. In 2015

THE WEEKND AND NFTs

On March 26, 2021, The Weeknd tweeted, "new song living in NFT space. coming soon. . ."[5] Non-fungible tokens (NFTs) are pieces of data representing the ownership of unique digital objects, such as songs, videos, and pieces of artwork. An NFT cannot be copied, but it can be sold or traded. Other musical acts, such as Kings of Leon and Grimes, have also participated in NFTs. The Weeknd's eight-piece NFT collection, which included a song, three audio-visual items, and four pieces of artwork, sold for a total of more than $2 million at auction. The song alone went for $490,000.[6]

The Weeknd's career has evolved in unique and unexpected ways during his long journey from the Toronto suburbs to the biggest stages on Earth.

Rolling Stone compiled a list of songs that would not exist without The Weeknd. Artists such as FKA Twigs, Swedish singer Tove Lo, and Drake are included in the breakdown.

The running theme throughout this music includes dark vibes, sexual overtones, and a hint of falsetto.

But before his sound could become pigeonholed, The Weeknd made the decision to collaborate with hitmakers like Max Martin. His duets with stars such as Ariana Grande introduced him to a wider audience. Meanwhile, Martin worked with The Weeknd to perfect the art of crafting monster pop hits. This combination of dark R&B mixed with slick pop songwriting has turned The Weeknd into an international superstar, capable of dominating the musical charts as well as headlining monumental live events like the Super Bowl halftime show. And his outspoken decision to withhold his music from consideration for the Grammys has been

HELPING HIS PARENTS' HOMELAND

On April 4, 2021, The Weeknd announced that he would be donating $1 million to aid in relief efforts for Ethiopia.[7] The money went toward the United Nations World Food Program, providing two million meals to Ethiopians in need. The Weeknd was horrified by the level of destruction inflicted on civilians and their villages due to ongoing conflict between the government in Ethiopia's capital, Addis Ababa, and the Tigray region of the country.

The Weeknd's larger-than-life Super Bowl halftime show demonstrated his ability to capture the imagination of millions with his songwriting and performing skills.

heralded by the media as an influence of change within the nomination systems.

Abel Tesfaye, better known as The Weeknd, continues to thrill audiences and keep musical critics guessing. His decision to give few interviews has often left many grasping for hidden meanings in his songs and pondering his next moves in the industry. Even today, The Weeknd has managed to hold on to some of the mystique that he developed years ago in Toronto. His commitment to his artistry has made a mark on the music business of today.

1990

The Weeknd is born Abel Tesfaye on February 16. He grows up in Scarborough, a suburb located east of Toronto, Ontario.

2011

In March, The Weeknd releases *House of Balloons*.

In July, The Weeknd plays his first live show, in Toronto, Canada.

In August, The Weeknd releases *Thursday*.

In December, The Weeknd releases *Echoes of Silence*.

2012

In April, The Weeknd makes his first appearance at Coachella and tours the United States.

In September, The Weeknd is signed by Universal Republic Records.

In November, *Trilogy* is released.

2013

In September, *Kiss Land* is released.

2014

In August, "Love Me Harder," a duet featuring The Weeknd and Ariana Grande, is released.

2015

The Weeknd makes a return to Coachella in the spring.

In August, *Beauty behind the Madness* is released.

2016

In January, The Weeknd receives an Oscar nomination for Best Original Song for "Earned It."

In November, *Starboy* is released.

2017

The Weeknd begins dating pop star Selena Gomez at the beginning of the year. By October, the couple has broken up.

2018

In March, *My Dear Melancholy* is released.

2020

In March, *After Hours* is released.

The Weeknd releases two Spanish-language remixes, one with Colombian singer Maluma and one with Spanish singer Rosalía.

2021

The Weeknd announces that he will boycott the Grammy Awards.

In February, The Weeknd performs at the Super Bowl LV halftime show.

FULL NAME

Abel Makkonen Tesfaye

DATE OF BIRTH

February 16, 1990

PLACE OF BIRTH

Toronto, Ontario, Canada

PARENTS

Makkonen and Samra Tesfaye

EDUCATION

West Hill Collegiate, Birchmount Park Collegiate
Scarborough, Ontario

CAREER HIGHLIGHTS

The Weeknd made an early appearance alongside Drake on "Crew Love" in 2012. The same year, he was signed to Universal Republic. The record label released *Trilogy*, a three-album set that included his previously self-released mixtapes, *House of Balloons*, *Thursday*, and *Echoes of Silence*. In 2013 *Kiss Land* was released. In 2015 he released *Beauty behind the Madness*. The album debuted at Number 1. In 2016 he was nominated for an Oscar for "Earned It." That same year he released *Starboy*, which debuted at Number 1. In 2020 he released *After Hours*, another Number 1 hit record. In 2021 he performed at the NFL's Super Bowl halftime show.

MIXTAPES, ALBUMS, AND EPs

House of Balloons (mixtape, 2011), *Thursday* (mixtape, 2011), *Echoes of Silence* (mixtape, 2011), *Trilogy* (compilation, 2012), *Kiss Land* (album, 2013), *Beauty behind the Madness* (album, 2015), *Starboy* (album, 2016), *My Dear Melancholy* (EP, 2018), *After Hours* (album, 2020)

CONTRIBUTION TO HIP-HOP

The Weeknd's dark and brooding sound made an impression on millennials, and it avoided falling into the standard sound of R&B's romantic crooners. As his music progressed and he crossed his mysterious vibe with pop, he became a fixture on mainstream radio and an international superstar.

CONFLICTS

The Weeknd's frequent references to drug use have been questioned by critics. He has also been criticized for his derogatory references to women, as well as those to the LGBTQ+ community. The Weeknd has had public squabbles with other artists, most notably Drake. He has been accused of not receiving permission to use samples from other artists, such as Portishead.

QUOTE

"I got into a lot of trouble, got kicked out of school, moved to different schools and finally dropped out. I really thought film was gonna be my way out, but I couldn't really make a movie to feel better, you know? Music was very direct therapy; it was immediate and people liked it. It definitely saved my life."

—*The Weeknd*

GLOSSARY

COLLABORATE
To work with someone else on a project.

CROONER
A singer who performs in a gentle, intimate manner.

DEROGATORY
Expressing a low opinion of someone or something; showing a lack of respect for someone or something.

EXTENDED PLAY (EP)
A musical recording of several songs, longer than a single but shorter than an album.

FALSETTO
An artificially high-pitched voice, especially in a man.

GENRE
A specific type of music, film, or writing.

MAINSTREAM
Ideas, attitudes, and activities that are considered normal.

MELANCHOLY
Depressive, brooding sadness.

MIXTAPE
A compilation of unreleased tracks, freestyle rap music, and DJ mixes of songs.

PAPARAZZI

Freelance photographers who take and sell photos of celebrities.

R&B

Rhythm and blues; a type of pop music of African American origin that has a soulful vocal style and features improvisation.

REMIX

A new and different version of a previous recording.

SAMPLE

A piece of recorded music used by DJs or producers to make new music.

SCALP

To attempt to sell a ticket to an event or performance, usually at a higher price than its face value.

SINGLE

A song or track released to the public independently of a complete album, which may or may not later be released as part of an album.

SOUNDTRACK

A collection of music that accompanies a film.

ADDITIONAL RESOURCES

SELECTED BIBLIOGRAPHY

Aswad, Jem. "The Weeknd Opens Up about His Past, Turning 30 and Getting Vulnerable on 'After Hours.'" *Variety*, 8 Apr. 2020, variety.com. Accessed 2 Apr. 2021.

Caramanica, John. "Can the Weeknd Turn Himself into the Biggest Pop Star in the World?" *New York Times*, 27 July 2015, nytimes.com. Accessed 1 May 2021.

Eells, Josh. "Sex, Drugs and R&B: Inside the Weeknd's Dark Twisted Fantasy." *Rolling Stone*, 21 Oct. 2015, rollingstone.com. Accessed 2 Apr. 2021.

FURTHER READINGS

Burling, Alexis. *Drake: Hip-Hop Superstar*. Abdo, 2018.

Kallen, Stuart A. *Rap and Hip-Hop*. ReferencePoint Press, 2019.

Wheeler, Jill C. *Travis Scott: Lo-Fi Hip-Hop Creator*. Abdo, 2020.

ONLINE RESOURCES

Booklinks
NONFICTION NETWORK
FREE! ONLINE NONFICTION RESOURCES

To learn more about The Weeknd, please visit **abdobooklinks.com** or scan this QR code. These links are routinely monitored and updated to provide the most current information available.

MORE INFORMATION

For more information on this subject, contact or visit the following organizations:

BILLBOARD
billboard.com

Billboard is a music magazine and website best known for its long-running charts ranking the popularity of songs and albums in a variety of genres. Its website features those charts as well as news and other information about the music industry.

REPUBLIC RECORDS
1755 Broadway
New York, NY 10019
republicrecords.com

Republic Records, owned by Universal Music Group, is The Weeknd's record label. Other artists signed to the label include Ariana Grande and Drake.

SOURCE NOTES

CHAPTER 1. THE WEEKND AT HALFTIME

1. Kevin Patra. "Official Attendance Expected for Super Bowl LV: 25,000 Fans, 30,000 Cutouts." *NFL*, 2 Feb. 2021, nfl.com. Accessed 27 July 2021.

2. Josh St. Clair. "The Weeknd Put $7 Million of His Own Money into His Super Bowl Halftime Performance." *Yahoo*, 7 Feb. 2021, yahoo.com. Accessed 27 July 2021.

3. Nick Brown. "13 Minutes, $13 Million: The Logistics of Pulling Off a Super Bowl Halftime Show." *Reuters*, 1 Feb. 2020, reuters.com. Accessed 27 July 2021.

4. John R. Kennedy. "The Weeknd Sees Sales Soar after Super Bowl." *iHeartRadio*, 9 Feb. 2021, iheartradio.ca. Accessed 27 July 2021.

5. Jackson Langford. "The Weeknd Says There Will Be No Special Guests at His Super Bowl Halftime Show." *NME*, 5 Feb. 2021, nme.com. Accessed 27 July 2021.

6. Heran Mamo. "The Weeknd's Super Bowl Halftime Show Won't Be as Bloody as His 'After Hours' Videos: 'I Definitely Want to Be Respectful.'" *Billboard*, 4 Feb. 2021, billboard.com. Accessed 27 July 2021.

7. Mamo, "The Weeknd's Super Bowl Halftime Show."

8. Gil Kaufman. "How the NFL Pulled Off a Safe Super Bowl LV Halftime Show in the Middle of a Pandemic." *Billboard*, 8 Feb. 2021, billboard.com. Accessed 27 July 2021.

9. Craig Jenkins. "So Now The Weeknd Is Our Collective Escape from Hell?" *Vulture*, 8 Feb. 2021, vulture.com. Accessed 27 July 2021.

CHAPTER 2. FROM THE SUBURBS OF TORONTO

1. Josh Eells. "Sex, Drugs and R&B: Inside the Weeknd's Dark Twisted Fantasy." *Rolling Stone*, 21 Oct. 2015, rollingstone.com. Accessed 27 July 2021.

2. Jem Aswad. "The Weeknd Opens Up about His Past, Turning 30 and Getting Vulnerable on 'After Hours.'" *Variety*, 8 Apr. 2020, variety.com. Accessed 27 July 2021.

3. Samuel Getachew. "How the 'Father of Ethiopian Jazz' Influenced The Weeknd." *Huffpost*, 9 Feb. 2017, huffintonpost.ca. Accessed 27 July 2021.

CHAPTER 3. THREE LITTLE MIXTAPES

1. Josh Eells. "Sex, Drugs and R&B: Inside the Weeknd's Dark Twisted Fantasy." *Rolling Stone*, 21 Oct. 2015, rollingstone.com. Accessed 27 July 2021.

CHAPTER 4. A NEW CHAPTER

1. Tom Goodwyn. "The Weeknd Covers Michael Jackson as He Plays His Debut UK Show—Video." *NME*, 8 June 2012, nme.com. Accessed 27 July 2021.

2. Josh Eells. "Sex, Drugs and R&B: Inside the Weeknd's Dark Twisted Fantasy." *Rolling Stone*, 21 Oct. 2015, rollingstone.com. Accessed 27 July 2021.

3. James Montgomery. "The Weeknd Speaks: How *Kiss Land* Tells the Story of His 'Second Chapter.'" *MTV News*, 11 Sept. 2013, mtv.com. Accessed 27 July 2021.

4. Tom Breihan. "The Weeknd—'Belong to the World' Video." *Stereogum*, 15 July 2013, stereogum.com. Accessed 27 July 2021.

5. @jetfury. "Seems @theweeknd have said there is no sample used or enough likeness to Machine Gun to warrant any infringement....or credit." *Twitter*, 17 July 2013, 5:25 a.m., twitter.com.

6. Ian Cohen. "The Weeknd: *Kiss Land*." *Pitchfork*, 9 Sept. 2013, pitchfork.com. Accessed 27 July 2021.

7. Chris Payne. "The Weeknd, 'Kiss Land': Track-by-Track Review." *Billboard*, 6 Sept. 2013, billboard.com. Accessed 27 July 2021.

8. Eells, "Sex, Drugs and R&B."

CHAPTER 5. BLOWING UP

1. "Behind the Scenes – The Weeknd 'Earned It' (Fifty Shades of Grey) Video." *YouTube*, uploaded by Republic Records, 21 Jan. 2015, youtube.com. Accessed 27 Aug. 2021.

2. Stacy Lambe. "Composer Stephan Moccio on Why The Weeknd's 'Earned It' Wasn't a Sure Thing." *ET*, 11 Feb. 2016, etonline.com. Accessed 27 July 2021.

3. Alex Gale. "The Weeknd Closes Coachella Saturday with Breakthrough Performance." *Billboard*, 12 Apr. 2015, billboard.com. Accessed 27 July 2021.

4. Kevin Lynch. "The Weeknd Rocks the Guinness World Records 2017 Edition with Two New Titles." *Guinness World Records*, 29 Aug. 2016, guinnessworldrecords.com. Accessed 27 July 2021.

5. Allison P. David. "The Weeknd: A Pop Star for the Demon Hours." *Esquire*, 25 Aug. 2020, esquire.com. Accessed 27 July 2021.

6. Bruce Britt. "The Oral History of The Weeknd's 'Beauty Behind the Madness.'" *Medium*, 13 Feb. 2016, medium.com. Accessed 27 July 2021.

7. Andrew Ryce. "The Weeknd: *Beauty Behind the Madness*." *Pitchfork*, 2 Sept. 2015, pitchfork.com. Accessed 27 July 2021.

8. Jon Dolan. "Beauty Behind the Madness." *Rolling Stone*, 10 Sept. 2015, rollingstone.com. Accessed 27 July 2021.

CHAPTER 6. LIVING IN THE SPOTLIGHT

1. Khari. "The Weeknd Hints at His Next Album Release." *The Source*, 13 Mar. 2016, thesource.com. Accessed 27 July 2021.

2. Edward Roberts. "The Weeknd Pulls Out of Rihanna's ANTI World Tour in Shock Move." *Mirror*, 23 Mar. 2016, mirror.co.uk. Accessed 27 July 2021.

3. Annie Zaleski. "The Weeknd's Resonant *Starboy* Embraces the Downside of Fame." *AV Club*, 28 Nov. 2016, avclub.com. Accessed 27 July 2021.

4. Frank Guan. "The Weeknd's *Starboy* Is One Long Winning Streak." *Vulture*, 5 Dec. 2016, vulture.com. Accessed 27 July 2021.

5. Mosi Reeves. "Review: The Weeknd's 'Starboy' Treads Murky Water in Innovative R&B Era." *Rolling Stone*, 28 Nov. 2016, rollingstone.com. Accessed 27 July 2021.

6. Kara Brown. "The Weeknd on Fame, Love and 'Melancholy.'" *Time*, 17 May 2018, time.com. Accessed 27 July 2021.

7. Brown, "The Weeknd on Fame, Love and 'Melancholy.'"

8. Tirhakah Love. "Review: The Weeknd's 'My Dear Melancholy' Mixes Deep Gloom and Tough Love." *Rolling Stone*, 2 Apr. 2018, rollingstone.com. Accessed 27 July 2021.

SOURCE NOTES

CHAPTER 7. WORKING WITH EVERYONE

1. Jem Aswad. "The Weeknd Recalls Working with Daft Punk: 'They're One of the Reasons I Make Music.'" *Variety*, 23 Feb. 2021, variety.com. Accessed 27 July 2021.

2. Candace McDuffie. "The Weeknd's Singles, Ranked." *Entertainment Weekly*, 6 Mar. 2020, ew.com. Accessed 27 July 2021.

CHAPTER 8. *AFTER HOURS* AND BEYOND

1. Tracy E. Gilchrist. "The Weeknd's 'Lost in the Fire' Feeds Into Violence against Bi Women." *Advocate*, 14 Jan. 2019, advocate.com. Accessed 28 July 2021.

2. @theweeknd. "TONIGHT WE START A BRAIN MELTING PSYCHOTIC CHAPTER LET'S GOOOO." *Twitter*, 26 Nov. 2019, 2:29 p.m., twitter.com.

3. Katie Bain. "The Weeknd on the Crew That Boosted Him from 'Basically Homeless' to the Super Bowl." *Billboard*, 28 Jan. 2021, billboard.com. Accessed 28 July 2021.

4. Jem Aswad. "The Weeknd: 'I Will No Longer Allow My Label to Submit My Music to the Grammys.'" *Variety*, 11 Mar. 2021, variety.com. Accessed 28 July 2021.

5. "Forbes Releases 2017 Celebrity 100 List of the World's Highest-Paid Entertainers." *Forbes*, 12 June 2017, forbes.com. Accessed 28 July 2021.

6. Howard Walker. "Home of the Week: Inside The Weeknd's Gorgeous $25 Million LA Mansion." *Robb Report*, 23 June 2020, robbreport.com. Accessed 28 July 2021.

7. "The Weeknd's Incredible Homes." *Love Property*, n.d., loveproperty.com. Accessed 28 July 2021.

CHAPTER 9. THE MOMENTUM CONTINUES

1. Jem Aswad. "The Weeknd Drops Hints about 'Beautiful' New Music." *Variety*, 4 May 2021, variety.com. Accessed 28 July 2021.

2. Jem Aswad. "The Weeknd Calls Grammys 'Corrupt.'" *Variety*, 3 May 2021, variety.com. Accessed 28 July 2021.

3. Malik Peay. "A Look Inside Our Zine with The Weeknd." *TMRW*, 16 Dec. 2020, tmrwmagazine.com. Accessed 28 July 2021.

4. Glenn Rowley. "The Weeknd Reveals Next Album Will Be Inspired by Pandemic, Black Lives Matter Movement." *Billboard*, 30 Dec. 2020, billboard.com. Accessed 28 July 2021.

5. @theweeknd. "new song living in NFT space. coming soon..." *Twitter*, 26 Mar. 2021, 2:01 p.m., twitter.com.

6. Rosie Perper, "The Weeknd's Limited-Edition NFT Collection Raises Over $2 Million USD." *Hypebeast*, 5 Apr. 2021, hypebeast.com. Accessed 28 July 2021.

7. Ellise Shafer. "The Weeknd Donates US $1 Million to Relief Efforts in Ethiopia." *CTV News*, 4 Apr. 2021, ctvnews.ca. Accessed 28 July 2021.

INDEX

ERIN NICKS

Erin Nicks has been a professional writer for more than 20 years. She has written for newspapers and websites, and she is the author of more than 20 books. She is originally from Thunder Bay, Ontario, Canada, and currently resides in Ottawa, Ontario.